Big
Jake

Big
Jake

Dave and Pat Sargent

Illustrated by
Blaine Sapaugh

Ozark Publishing, Inc.
P.O. Box 389
Redfield, Arkansas 72132

F

Sar   Sargent, Dave

      Big Jake, by Dave and Pat Sargent. Illus. by
Blaine Sapaugh.

      Ozark Publishing, Inc., 1993.

      49P. illus. (Animal Pride Series)

      Summary: Big Jake is a tough little mouse
who has a narrow escape.

      1. Mice. I. Sargent, Pat. II. Title. III. Series.

ISBN Casebound 1-56763-030-8

ISBN Paperback 1-56763-029-4

Ozark Publishing, Inc.

P.O. Box 389, 439 Rhoads Rd.

Redfield, AR 72132

Ph: 1-800-321-5671

Printed in the United States of America

Inspired by

the thousands of field mice that lived in
the fields on our farm.

Dedicated to

Charlie Hollingsworth of Magnet Cove
Elementary School.

Foreword

Jake is a little mouse who is very curious. One day he is caught in the open by a chicken hawk.

Contents

Big
Jake

One

New Home

Mama and Daddy Mouse watched the new hay barn going up. They watched with a great deal of interest. They were trying to decide the exact spot they wanted for their new home. They usually slept during the warm spring days, but after the terrible storm last week, they had no home. The storm had completely washed away the nest they had shared for the past six months, and now they were looking for a new place.

Mama Mouse watched as Farmer John nailed the last board on the back side of the barn. She woke Daddy Mouse and, tugging at his front leg, begged, "Come on, Morse, let's check out the loft. That's where I want our new home–in the hayloft."

Morse opened his black beady eyes and surveyed the almost finished barn. It sure was high! It would make a fine home for Matilda and the little ones that would soon be arriving.

Matilda scampered toward the barn, then stopped and looked back to see if Morse was coming. When she couldn't see him, she hurried back to find him.

Morse was dozing off again, wishing Matilda would let him be. She twitched her nose and said, "That beats all I've ever seen! It's almost time for my babies to be born and just look at their father! He doesn't seem to care! I'll just have to take care of things myself–as usual!"

She scampered across the field to the new hay barn and, without a

moment's hesitation, shot through the door and up the walls to the loft!

Matilda stopped dead still in her tracks, then threw her front feet up to her face and said, "Oh, no! There's no hay! How will I ever get my nest built in time?"

After making her way back to the edge of the woods, she began a frantic search for bird feathers and fur. She knew exactly where to find the fur. She headed straight for the blackberry thicket that was about

4

fifty yards south of the new barn.

When Matilda reached the blackberry thicket, she began gathering fur from the thorns on the bushes. The thorns had pulled the fur from the rabbits and other furry animals that had either lived in the thicket or had taken refuge there.

Carrying as much fur as she could hold in her mouth, she made trip after trip to the loft of the new hay barn. After she had placed all the fur in a pile in the corner of the loft, she went searching for small feathers.

She gathered enough feathers to shape her nest and spent the next hour or so lining it with fur. When she finished, she stood back and admired her work. A deep sigh escaped her lips. She knew she had done a fine job. She crawled into the nest and made several turns before curling up for a much-needed nap.

Farmer John's noisy tractor woke Matilda. It sounded like it was coming right into her nest with her. Suddenly a bale of hay landed on the floor of the loft with a thud and a bounce! Matilda squeaked and took off running just as the bale settled next to her nest!

She crouched close to the wall the entire time Farmer John was tossing the bales of hay into the loft. Then, to her surprise, Farmer John jumped down from the trailer

that he had backed into the barn
and started up the ladder to the loft.
،

Matilda darted from bale to
bale while Farmer John neatly
stacked the hay in front of her nest.
She knew she must not let him see
her. She watched as he pulled a
handkerchief from his back pocket,
removed his straw hat, and wiped
his brow.

Farmer John climbed down
the ladder and up onto his tractor,

and Matilda jumped as he started it up. After the sound of the tractor died away, she made her way to her nest. It was completely hidden by the bales of hay, which offered even more security and comfort. Just as she settled in, she felt a sharp twinge and knew it was time–time for her babies to be born.

Minutes later, after carrying her babies in her tummy for only eighteen days, Matilda looked down and started counting, "One, two, three, four, five, six, seven. My word! I have seven new mouths to feed!"

Looking around the big hayloft, she said, "At least I have a nice roomy place to raise them. They'll have lots of room to run and play, and with all the insects, leaves, seeds, and stems of plants, they'll have plenty to eat. I feel very fortunate."

Well, while Matilda was admiring her little pink, furless babies, Ole Barney, the Bear Killer, trotted into the new barn to check it out. He sniffed all around, then stopped when he came to the ladder that led to the loft. His nose wiggled; he smelled a mouse!

Barney placed his front feet on the ladder and stretched his long neck toward the loft. When he barked softly, Matilda almost jumped out of her skin! She wondered if that old hound dog could climb ladders! She quietly made her way to the edge of the loft and peeked over.

Down below, Barney first saw Matilda's long, narrow nose with whiskers on it; then he saw her beady little eyes looking down at him. Then he saw something else. He saw fear in her eyes. At that exact moment, he caught the special smell that newborn animals give off, and he knew Matilda must have some new babies.

Barney growled a low warning growl. He knew Farmer John would not want mice living in his new hay barn. Mice gnawed on wood with their chisel-like teeth, and they made holes in walls that other animals could crawl through. And if Farmer John decided to store wheat in the new barn, the mice would eat the wheat and scatter it all over the floor.

Since Barney had no way of

getting to the mice, he gave one last growl as if to say, "I'll find a way of getting you out of here, and in the meantime, you'd better not mess up anything." Then, Ole Barney turned and trotted out the door and turned in the direction of the house.

Two

Chicken Hawk

Matilda scurried back to her nest and counted her babies to make sure they were all there. She knew Barney hadn't bothered her babies, but his very presence made her uneasy. Barney knew that she and her babies were living in the hayloft, and after hearing all the animals talk about Barney and how he had killed that old grizzly bear, Matilda didn't feel so safe anymore. She didn't feel safe at all.

About ten days later, soft fur covered the baby mice, and Matilda already knew which child was going to give her the most trouble. It was the one who was bigger than all the others–the one she called Big Jake.

Big Jake's legs were just a little bit longer, his head was a little larger, and his body was a little fatter than the others. This was because he was always nursing. Every time Matilda lay down, Big Jake wanted to eat!

After almost two weeks had gone by, Matilda woke up one day to see two beady little black eyes staring her right in the face. It startled her so that she jumped straight

up in her bed. She gasped and said, "Oh, thank heavens! It's only you, Big Jake! I was dreaming about that old hound dog and just knew he had figured out a way to climb that ladder."

Big Jake wiggled his nose and

said, "You must be my mama. I can tell by the way you smell."

Matilda smiled and nodded her head. Now that Big Jake's eyes were open, she figured he would be all over the place–not still a second during his waking hours. She pointed to her other babies and said, "These are your brothers and sisters, Big Jake. You are the biggest, so you must help me take care of them."

Big Jake looked at the others and thought to himself, "They can take care of themselves. I'm going hunting. I'm hungry." And with food on his mind, he wobbled over to the edge of the loft and swayed back and forth, losing his balance.

Big Jake might have fallen, but

Matilda was there in a flash. She reached out and grabbed his tail with her sharp teeth and hung on tightly.

Big Jake squealed. "Ouch, Mama! That hurts!"

Matilda carried Big Jake over to the nest and put him down. She said, "Don't go near the edge of the loft until you can walk better. If you fall to the ground below, it will hurt you."

Matilda had no sooner gotten the words out of her mouth when Big Jake made another dash for the edge of the hayloft. He gave the ladder a glance, then, teetering and tottering and reeling and rocking, he made his way to the ground below.

Having reached the ground safely, Big Jake explored the huge barn. He looked in all four corners and walked along three walls, looking for something to eat. He also searched in the middle of the barn, but he found nothing–nothing at all that even smelled as good as his mama's milk tasted. He was about to head for the ladder when he noticed a big hole in one of the walls. Actually, it wasn't a hole at all. It was an open door. And as quick as a cat can wink its eye, Big Jake made a dash for the great outdoors.

Matilda had been watching from up above, and when she saw Big Jake run outside, she threw her front feet up to her face and exclaimed, "Mercy me! A hawk will get that boy for sure!" She scampered to the edge of the loft, and without bothering to use the ladder, she half-climbed, half-slid down the side of the wall. When she reached the door, Big Jake was nowhere in sight.

Matilda saw a giant shadow cross the ground. Instinctively, she ran back inside the barn. Just then she heard Big Jake's loud, frightened squeak, and she knew that a hawk or an owl or something was after him.

Matilda made a dash for the door. She knew what she must do. She must sacrifice herself so that Big Jake might live. She figured the hawk or owl or whatever it was would prefer a big mouse to a little mouse and would eat her instead of her little Big Jake.

Another loud squeak and then a squawk reached Matilda's ears, and she knew by those sounds that Big Jake was cornered. Finally, she saw him. He was standing with his back against a tree. His body was tense, and his little black beady eyes were glowing! Big Jake was mad!

Matilda slid to a halt beside Big Jake. When he saw his mama, he said, "Get behind me, Mama. I'll protect you!" Then he asked, "Mama, what is that thing?"

Searching the sky with her frightened eyes, Matilda saw the hawk circling to make another attack. "It's a hawk!" she answered.

"Come on, Jake, run!" She grabbed Big Jake and half-pulled, half-shoved him under a nearby blackberry thicket.

Big Jake tumbled head over heels! When he finally stopped, he ran to the edge of the thicket and peeked out. The hawk had evidently given up, because it flew over the barn, made a circle, then disappeared behind the trees.

Big Jake sat perfectly still. He wasn't about to move–not until

his mama told him it was okay.

Matilda scampered to the edge of the blackberry thicket and searched the sky and nearby trees with her eyes, knowing full well that the hawk could be sitting on a limb just waiting for the two frightened mice to emerge from their hiding places.

Big Jake was scared but excited! He wanted to explore some more, and Matilda had a hard time keeping him still.

Finally, after ten long minutes had passed, Matilda said, "Big Jake, when I say go, I want you to run as fast as you can back to the barn! And don't stop on the floor below. You must run up the ladder or up the wall and crawl into our nest. Do you understand?"

Big Jake had a puzzled look on his face. He asked, "What's a barn, Mama?"

Matilda threw her front feet to her face and exclaimed, "Mercy me, Jake! The barn I'm talking about is that big red building right over there. That's where our nest is. Our nest is in the hayloft of the barn. The barn is our home. You must look at it closely and remember what it looks like, because whenever you come out to play or hunt for food, you must remember what home looks like."

Big Jake looked the barn over, then said, "Okay, Mama. I'm ready!"

Matilda's eyes swept the sky and the trees, and when she didn't see the hawk, she yelled, "Go!"

Big Jake scampered as fast as he could across the open space between the blackberry thicket in the edge of the woods and the big red barn that sat on the edge of the field. Matilda crouched in the edge of the thicket and watched until Big Jake ran safely through the barn door, then she made a dash for the barn. When she reached the barn, Big Jake was trying desperately to climb the ladder.

Matilda ran up the wall, then scampered over to the ladder to give Big Jake encouragement. After a great deal of climbing and

slipping and climbing and slipping, he finally made his way to the loft. Big Jake and Matilda made their way to the back corner of the loft to their nest. And there, in the nest, were twelve little black beady eyes looking at them.

Matilda said, "Would you look at that! Your brothers' and sisters' eyes are finally open."

Big Jake squeaked. "Come on! Let's go play!" he said.

Three

Tractor Ride

Jake scampered toward the ladder, then stopped and looked back to see if his brothers and sisters were following him. They were nowhere in sight. Being a very adventurous little mouse, Jake teetered and tottered and half-slid down the ladder, thinking, "They're no fun. I'll play by myself."

About that time, Jake heard the tractor coming. He darted behind a box on the ground under Farmer John's workbench that was attached to the west wall of the barn.

Farmer John backed the hay wagon into the barn, then jumped down off the tractor and, going to the back of the wagon, started picking up the bales and stacking them against the back wall.

Jake peeked out from behind the box, watching Farmer John's every move. Then his eyes focused

on the hay wagon. The loose hay on the wagon looked inviting, and Jake was really tired. He waited until Farmer John picked up a bale of hay and turned to place it against the wall, then he scampered as fast as his little legs could carry him to the wagon. He quickly ran up the rubber tire, then scratched and clawed his way up onto the wagon bed. Darting around the end of the bales, Jake made his way to the front of the wagon and, digging down under the loose hay, curled up into a little round ball and was soon fast asleep.

Big Jake was so tired from all the excitement of being chased by the hawk and his struggle to climb back up the ladder to his nest that he didn't hear the tractor start up. He didn't feel the gentle sway of the hay wagon, either, when Farmer John drove his tractor pulling the wagon to the house for lunch.

Some time later, Jake opened his eyes and looked around. "What was all that jiggling and bouncing?" he wondered. To his total amazement, he saw three things that looked somewhat like Farmer

John jumping up and down on the
hay wagon, throwing loose hay on
one another.

Farmer John's daughters were
having a big time playing on the
hay wagon. They had no idea that
Big Jake was deep in the hay. That
is, not until he moved.

At the sight of the little mouse,
the three girls let out several squeals
that could be heard all through the
nearby woods. The squeals scared

Big Jake much more than the hawk had.

First, Jake ran to his left, then he ran to his right. No matter which direction he ran, there always seemed to be two chubby little hands reaching for him. He had never seen so many little hands!

Jake's heart almost stopped when something soft and warm closed around him and he felt himself being lifted into the air.

April yelled, "I've got him! I've got him!" and the other girls gathered around wanting to see the little mouse.

Over the next few weeks the girls fed Big Jake some of the milk and cheese and crumbs Ole Barney had left in his dish. They didn't try to pick him up again, so he soon learned to trust them. He liked to climb into April's doll carriage for a nap, and one day, when the girls were strolling down the lane that went right past the new hay barn, Big Jake opened his eyes and crawled out from under the doll blanket. When he placed his front feet on the edge of the carriage and looked over, he saw Mama Mouse and six young mice huddled at the corner of the big red barn.

Suddenly, a picture flashed through his mind–the picture of a little tiny mouse with black beady eyes and a big hawk swooping down from the sky. Big Jake knew where he was.

Wandering further from the farmhouse than they had ever walked before, the girls had unknowingly brought Big Jake back home.

He let out a squeak and jumped from the doll carriage. The girls watched wide-eyed as Jake scampered to the corner of the barn where the other mice were.

Matilda nudged Big Jake several times with her nose, welcoming him home, and then she asked him where he had been.

Jake told his mama and his brothers and sisters all about his adventures. He talked for hours! Finally, Matilda smiled and said to herself, "Big Jake is not only the biggest, but he also has the biggest mouth!"

Mouse Facts

A mouse is a small animal with soft fur, a pointed snout, round black eyes, rounded ears, and a thin tail. The word "mouse" is not the name of any one kind of animal or family of animals. Many kinds of rodents (gnawing animals) are called mice. They include small rats, hamsters, gerbils, jerboas, lemmings, voles, harvest mice, deer mice, and grasshopper mice. All these animals have chisel-like front teeth that are useful for gnawing. A rodent's front teeth grow throughout the animal's life.

There are hundreds of kinds of mice, and they live in most parts of the world. They can be found in the mountains, in fields and woodlands, in swamps, near streams, and in deserts. Probably the best-known kind of mouse is the house mouse. It lives wherever people live, and often builds its nests in homes, garages, or barns. Some kinds of white house mice are raised as pets. Other kinds are used by scientists to learn about sickness, to test new drugs, and to study behavior.

House mice probably could be found in the homes of people who lived during ancient times. Those mice probably stole the people's food, just as mice do today. The word "mouse" comes from an old Sanskrit word meaning thief. Sanskrit is an ancient language of Asia, where scientists believe house mice originated. House mice spread from Asia throughout Europe. The ancestors of the house mice that now live in North and South America were brought there by English, French, and Spanish ships during the 1500s.

House mice always seem to be busy. Those that live in buildings may scamper about day or night. House mice that live in fields and forests usually come out only at night. All house mice climb well and can often be heard running between the walls of houses.

The body of a house mouse is two and one-half to three and one-half inches long without the tail.

The tail is the same length or a little shorter. Most house mice weigh one-half to one ounce. Their size and weight, and the length of their tails, differ greatly among the many varieties and even among individuals of the same variety.

The fur of most house mice is soft, but it may be stiff and wiry. It is grayish-brown on the animal's back and sides, and yellowish-white underneath. House mice raised as pets or for use in laboratories may have pure white fur, black or brown spots, or other combinations of colors. The tail is covered by scaly skin.

A house mouse has a small head and a long, narrow snout. Several long, thin whiskers grow from the sides of the snout. These whiskers, like those of a cat, help the mouse feel its way in the dark. The animal has rounded ears, and its eyes look somewhat like round black beads. A mouse can hear well, but it has poor vision. Probably because house mice cannot see well, they may enter a lighted room even if people are there.

Like all other rodents, mice

have strong, sharp front teeth that grow throughout the animal's life. With these chisel-like teeth, mice can gnaw holes in wood, tear apart packages to get at food inside, and damage books, clothing, and furniture.

A house mouse eats almost anything that human beings eat. It feeds on any meat or plant material that it can find. Mice also eat such household items as glue, leather, paste, and soap. House mice that live out-of-doors eat insects and the leaves, roots, seeds, and stems of plants. Mice always seem to be looking for something to eat, but they need little food. They damage much more food than they eat.

House mice live wherever

they can find food and shelter. Any dark place that is warm and quiet makes an excellent home for mice. A mouse may build its nest in a warm corner of a barn, on a beam under the roof of a garage, or in a box stored in an attic or basement. The animal may tear strips of clothing or upholstery to get materials for its nest. It may line the nest with feathers or cotton stolen from pillows. House mice that live in fields or woodlands dig holes in the ground and build nests of grass inside. They may line the nests with feathers or pieces of fur.

A female house mouse may give birth every twenty to thirty days. She carries her young in her body for eighteen to twenty-one days before they are born. She has four to seven young at a time. Newborn mice have pink skin and no fur, and their eyes are closed. They are completely helpless. Soft fur covers their bodies by the time they are ten days old. When they are fourteen days old, their eyes open. Young mice stay near the nest for about three weeks after birth. Then they leave to build their own nests and start raising families. Most female house mice begin to have young when they are about forty-five days old.

People are probably the worst enemies of the house mouse. They set traps and place poisons where mice can easily find them. Almost every meat-eating animal is an enemy of house mice. Cats and dogs hunt mice in houses and barns. Coyotes, foxes, snakes, and other animals capture them in forests and woodlands. Owls, hawks, and other

birds of prey swoop down on them in fields and prairies. Rats and even other mice are also enemies. House mice may live as long as a year in a hidden corner of an attic or basement. But they have so many enemies that few wild mice survive more than two or three months. Some mice kept as pets or in laboratories may live six years.

House mice avoid their enemies by hiding. A mouse seldom wanders far from its nest. It spends most of its time within an area of about two hundred feet in diameter. Wherever possible, the mouse moves along paths protected by furniture, boxes, or other objects. The mouse scampers as fast as it can across the open spaces between the objects. House mice do not like water and try to avoid it, but they can swim.

Other books by
Dave and Pat Sargent

Big Jake